Jump into
the New

Written by Janis Mackay

Illustrated by Alfredo Belli

Collins

Chapter 1

"Pick me!" voices clamoured. Everyone wanted to be in Cody Mather's team. He was taller than most of the children in his class and had a confidence that made him the natural captain. He was also the only one with proper football boots and Esk Valley Rovers maroon football socks. He held the ball high, shouting how they were all to get into their positions.

"Let's go! Go! Go!" he yelled.

"What about the new boy?" Morven asked. She was the captain of the other team. She nodded towards the boy standing alone at the side of the pitch.

He'd been in school a few months, but was still called the new boy, mostly because people couldn't remember his name.

"It would make it uneven," Cody said, throwing the ball in the air. "And, hey, he's not even got trainers on. Plus, he's not got a clue. He seriously messed up the basketball game last time, remember?"

Who could forget? He'd run with the ball like it was rugby!

The game began. Cody was the best player by far. He kicked to Marty who passed to Sam. Morven tried to tackle Sam but not before Sam kicked the ball back to Cody. Team Morven's goalie, Angus, was shifting nervously from foot to foot, watching Cody get closer.

"Pass it here!" Ravi shouted and Cody, dodging Jasmin, kicked the ball to Ravi who slammed the ball into the net. Team Cody cheered like this was Scotland winning the World Cup and not a school breaktime game.

The boy on the sideline cheered too. When Cody glanced over, the boy looked away, to where a group of younger pupils were playing tag.

Angus clutched the ball protectively.

"Kick it up the field!" Cody shouted, gesturing for him to get a move on. "Come on, come on, come on, we've not got much time."

Angus kicked the ball but Cody quickly intercepted, then passed to Max who dribbled it down the field. Max passed to Shuna who smashed the ball into the net. It was two-nil for team Cody and Angus looked miserable.

Soon it looked like it would be three-nil. Cody was steaming up the pitch, then he passed to Max who kicked hard. Angus gaped in wonder as the ball glanced off the goalpost, sailed off the pitch and rolled to where the new boy was standing.

He took his chance and kicked the ball, running on to the pitch after it. Cody was yelling for him to get off, but the new boy kept going, dribbling the ball. He appeared to be in Morven's team, as he was heading in that direction.

Morven called for him to kick the ball to her, but he seemed to be a one-boy act.

"Pass it here!" Millie shouted. But the new boy was lining up the ball, looking ready to slam it into the net, when Cody tackled him to the ground.

"It's a team game!" Cody yelled. "Do you know what that means?"

The boy was lying on the ground, red in the face, staring up at Cody and looking like he might burst into tears. "No … I mean, yes … I mean, I don't know!"

"Yeah, well, that's pretty obvious!"

Whatever else Cody said was drowned out by the clamour of the bell ringing for the end of breaktime.

No one noticed when the new boy didn't reappear in class.

Even the teacher didn't seem to notice. "Here's your project for the summer holidays," she said, flashing onto the whiteboard the bright orange words – *Holiday Time* – and a smiley face with a speech bubble, urging them to *Jump into the new!* "On your summer holidays," she explained, "I want you to try new things, taste new food, meet new people, go to new places, then come back and tell us all about it." Knowing Cody was off to the Costa Brava, she suggested he could learn new Spanish words.

Cody smiled. This time next week they'd be in Spain. He couldn't wait! Then as soon as they were back, he was off again with school, for the outdoor adventure holiday in Aviemore. Then it would be the relaxing week in a chalet on the Isle of Skye, with a hot tub. He would have so many new things to talk about. A few Spanish words would just be the start of it!

Only then did the teacher seem to notice someone was missing. She picked up her register, frowning as she scanned the class. "Where's Alfie?"

Chapter 2

"I can't wait for Aviemore," Max said, swinging his rucksack and nudging Cody. "Do you want a top bunk or bottom?"

"Top, for sure," Cody said.

They were on their way home from school, Cody talking about all the new activities added this year, like zorbing, land yachting and go-karting.

"I want to be in your team for everything," Max said. "It's going to be ace."

"Sunny Spain first," Cody reminded him, flipping back his blond hair.

"Oh yeah." Max grinned. He was also going to Spain with his family.

Cody had reached his house, 17 Esk Avenue, and clocked his dad's car in the drive. "See you tomorrow, Max. Last day of school! Then the adventures begin!"

Max tore off down the street, hurling his rucksack into the air and catching it. Cody sauntered up the path. As soon as he opened the front door, he knew something was wrong.

"Mum?" No answer. "I'm home!" Still no answer. He felt his heart race. Something was up. There was no radio on. No smells of cooking. Cody stood in the hallway. He could hear murmured voices from the kitchen. He didn't immediately open the kitchen door and go through but stood there, as if turned to stone. He caught just one word. It was his dad speaking, his voice low and heavy. *"Ruined. Ruined".* He said it over and over. *"We're ruined!"* Cody wanted to turn and run after Max, and talk about land yachting, and kayaking. He wanted to be miles from whatever was happening here. He took a step back.

"Is that you, Cody?" His mum's voice, strained and nervous sounding. He heard a shuffle of feet. The kitchen door opened. Cody stared at his mum. She looked like she'd been crying. Her blonde hair, usually so neat, was a mess. Her eyes red. Her hands twisting together. Behind her, Cody could see his dad slumped at the kitchen table, his head in his hands.

"I'm sorry, son," his dad was saying. "I wanted to give you everything. I didn't mean for – "

"The business has crashed," his mum said, looking like she was struggling to hold back tears. "It might feel like the end of the world, but … it's … it's not. Might take a bit of getting used to, but – "

"What do you mean?" Cody snapped. He looked from his mum to his dad. "What are you talking about?"

His mum took a long intake of breath. "I mean, things will change."

"What things?"

"The summer plans for one. Things that cost money, because – " She sighed. "We don't have … as much as we used to."

His dad kept on muttering how sorry he was. How it was all such a terrible mess.

"What about Aviemore?" Cody couldn't believe what he was hearing. "Things *can't* change!"

"I'm really sorry, Cody. Your dad did everything he could to save the business, but it wasn't enough. So we need to pull in our belts."

Cody threw his rucksack on the kitchen floor. "So, like, we're *poor*?"

His parents didn't answer.

"So, like, all the plans for … summer – " Cody's voice trailed off. He could feel hot tears welling up.

"Are cancelled," his mum said, still twisting her hands. "We're so sor– "

Cody stormed off, slamming the front door. Tears were pricking his eyes now. He marched down Esk Avenue, then back. Fast walking felt like the only thing to do. He was ready to march down the street again, but suddenly he was afraid he might bump into Max Maclean. What would he tell him? That they were poor? He couldn't face his friends feeling sorry for him. So he crept back into the house, slipped into his bedroom and crawled into bed with his school clothes on. Never, in all his 12 years of life, had he felt so miserable.

Chapter 3

"It's not like losing your job," his mum was struggling to explain, "where you get redundancy money." Her hands cradled her coffee cup. Cody had no appetite for breakfast. And his dad was still in bed. "When you have your own business, you take risks. You can make a lot of money." She blew over the hot coffee. "And you can … lose a lot." She looked like she hadn't slept a wink. "An awful lot."

Cody didn't say anything. Half the long restless night he'd gone over and over in his mind what he would tell Max and the others. Now he pushed the bowl away, grabbed his rucksack and hurried from the kitchen.

"Enjoy your last day of term," his mum called after him, half-heartedly.

Cody grunted but didn't look back. He didn't grin and wave like he normally did – because nothing was normal anymore.

At morning break, by the football pitch, Cody blurted the words he'd been rehearsing. "So, poor dad, he's not well. Yeah, big shame. He has to take it easy. We're just going to hang about here. So boring. Until he gets better."

His friends were all staring at him.

"What?" Ravi frowned. "But what about Aviemore?"

"You have to come to Aviemore." That was Max.

"Totally," said Morven. "Your dad will be better by then."

"Might not be," Cody muttered, with a shrug.

Saved by the bell, he hurried back into class, where it was all abuzz with excitement, and the teacher reminding them to *Jump into the new.*

Being the last day of term, school finished at lunch time.
Normally Cody ate his packed lunch with the others by
the football pitch, then they would get a game, but today
he had no lunch, and no desire to be with the others.
They would want to know exactly what was wrong with
his dad and Cody hadn't worked out a suitable illness.
While everyone was throwing high fives and chanting how
they were all going on summer holidays, Cody snuck off.
He hurried away from the school gates, in the opposite
direction to home. Home felt like a sad place to be, and
Cody was in no hurry to get there.

Instead, he wandered the streets, then found himself near the park. He went in. It was busy with parents, buggies and young children, and noisy with a dog barking.

It had been a while since Cody had been to the park. He heard the creak – creak – creak of a swing. When the swings came into view, he saw a boy swinging, so high Cody thought he might go over the top bar. He was as high as the tree tops. Cody stared, mesmerised by the loud creaking and the daredevil swinging.

The last thing he expected was for the boy on the swing to shout his name. "Cody!" the boy yelled, as though he'd spotted his long-lost friend. "Hey, Cody!" The boy scuffed the ground with his feet and quickly the swing lost height and momentum. The boy beamed at Cody. It was the new boy. In a flash, Cody remembered his name: Alfie.

"You want to swing, Cody?" Alfie shouted, pulling the swing next to him, and gesturing enthusiastically for Cody to come and take it.

Cody didn't, not immediately. But what else was there to do? Shrugging, he ambled over to the swing, and all the while, Alfie was smiling widely, looking as excited as Cody looked miserable.

"These swings are the best," Alfie said, "better than the ones in Manchester, and the ones in Glasgow. When you go really high, you can see Edinburgh, and that big hill. It's huge, like a mountain."

"Arthur's Seat," Cody muttered.

"Who?"

"The big hill," Cody went on, beginning to push himself. "It's called Arthur's Seat."

Chapter 4

The next morning, Alfie was in the park early. A few joggers
were about, and a good few dog-walkers too, hurling
sticks and brightly coloured balls. Alfie pushed himself
round for a while on the roundabout, then he went down
the slide. But mostly he kept glancing towards the big grey
iron gates. He didn't want to miss Cody. The day before
had been great. Even though Cody hadn't said much, they
had hung out together. And when Alfie had asked him
to come back the next day, Cody had shrugged, like he
actually might.

Alfie was glad it was now the school holidays.
He didn't have to hide in the bushes, pretending he
was at school when he wasn't. He was also glad it was
the summer solstice. He knew because his dad had
told him before he headed off for work that morning.
"It means the longest day of the year," his dad had said,
stretching his arms wide. Alfie wanted to tell Cody about
the summer solstice.

"Way up in the far north, it doesn't get dark at this time,"
his dad had said, when they sat eating hot buttered
toast together. "You remember it up there, don't you, son?"

Alfie nodded, though the truth was he didn't remember clearly. He'd only been five when his parents had split up and he and his dad left the far north. "I remember it was windy. Or maybe that was Glasgow."

His dad laughed. "Wick and Glasgow, both pretty windy. It's better here." His dad stood up and reached for his hard hat.

"So, can we stay here?"

His dad gave him that lopsided sorry smile. "You know I have to go where the work is, son. But we're here for a wee while. Enjoy it, eh?"

Alfie nibbled his toast and didn't say anymore. He knew all the answers. How construction isn't like other jobs. Houses get built, then the builders move on to the next building site.

"Ella will be here soon," his dad said. "It's fine to go to the park, but pop back and say hello." His dad grinned. Ella was his second cousin who had agreed to spend the school holidays sitting in their flat, working on her computer and keeping an eye on Alfie.

Alfie nodded as his dad quickly made sandwiches for them all, then paused at the door. "Look, Alfie, I'll take a few days off in July, and we can do stuff together, OK? Like, go fishing, bird watching, yeah?"

"It's OK, I've got a new friend," Alfie blurted out. He hadn't meant to but out it came, proud.

"That's great, son. You enjoy your day." And his dad was gone, greeting Ella on his way out. Two minutes later Alfie was on his way to the park to wait for his new friend.

It seemed like hours Alfie was in the park. Parents with younger children came and went. The sun climbed up the sky. Alfie ate his cheese and pickle sandwiches. He drank his carton of orange juice. When he was sure his new friend wasn't coming, the excitement fizzed out of him.

Alfie was on the swing, scuffing his feet, thinking how he would go home and watch TV, when he saw two feet appear in front of him, sporting dark red proper football socks.

"Want to kick a ball?"

Alfie looked up. Cody had come back and was holding a football under his arm. Alfie jumped off the swing. "Sure."

Cody strode away from the swings. Alfie, the smaller of the two, ran to keep up.

"Great you came," Alfie shouted. Cody didn't say anything but, reaching an open stretch of ground, he set the ball down. "It's the solstice," Alfie yelled.

Only then did Cody, with one foot on the ball, look at him. "What?"

"The longest day of the year." Alfie stretched his arms wide like his dad had done.

The day I should be on a plane flying to Spain, Cody didn't say, but the thought weighed on his mind. "Here!" he shouted, kicking the ball towards Alfie. "Passing practice. Now kick it back to me."

Back and forth they kicked the ball, and Alfie couldn't keep the smile off his face. "This is ace!" he yelled, even though most of the time his kicks didn't go where he meant them to. "Every time I try to join a team, my dad gets a new job and we move."

Cody stared at him.

"I mean, I'm always the new boy," Alfie explained, pointing to the slow rolling ball, like being the new boy was the reason his kicking wasn't great.

Cody lifted the ball and brushed grass off it. "So, like, how many schools have you been to?"

Alfie counted on his fingers. "Seven."

"I've been to one school," Cody said. He set the ball down again, then kicked it towards Alfie.

Alfie missed and had to run after the ball. Running back with it, he set it down like Cody had done, then frowning with concentration, he kicked it towards his new friend. "You're lucky," he called.

"Ha!" Cody laughed bitterly. "You don't know anything. I have to be the unluckiest boy around." He kicked the ball back hard. Alfie dived for the ball and caught it in his arms.

"OK," Cody said, "let's practise scoring."

For the next hour or so, they shot goals. Alfie wanted the game to never end. He was a better saver than a scorer, and Cody said maybe he would pick him for the team next year.

"If I'm still here," Alfie said, glumly. "We don't stay around much, worse luck."

They both looked up then, at a long white line made in the blue sky by a droning plane. Cody slumped his shoulders and sat on the ball. "I shouldn't even be here," he muttered.

Alfie waited for him to say more but Cody just stared morosely up at the distant plane.

"Well, I'm glad you're here," Alfie said.

Cody jumped up and grabbed his ball. "Well, I'm not. I'm not glad one bit!" With that he stomped off.

Alfie jumped up. "Hey, Cody, will you come back tomorrow?"

Cody didn't answer, didn't want to show the tears stinging his eyes.

"I'll be here," Alfie yelled. "We can do more goals. Or other stuff. We can even go to the river. See ducks, go fishing!"

Then Cody was gone. A dog ran over to Alfie, barking excitedly. Alfie held the dog by the collar, waiting while an old man hobbled after it.

"Thanks, son," the man said, sounding breathless as he clipped the lead. "He's too much for me."

Alfie watched them go, then headed home, feeling hungry. His dad would be in soon. Alfie tried to remember what day it was. Realising it was Thursday, he quickened his pace. Macaroni cheese day.

Cody's family were also having macaroni cheese. Not steak like they used to. Not a big salad. But plain and simple macaroni cheese. If this was being poor, Cody thought, scooping up the cheesy pasta, maybe it wasn't too terrible. Maybe they could eat this every night.

"At least we got the deposit back from the chalet on Skye," his mum said, pushing her uneaten food away. She reached over and patted her son's arm. "We could go for a walk tomorrow if you like?"

Cody surprised himself, but out it came. "Na, it's fine. I've got a friend and I'm teaching him football in the park. So I've got things to do. Don't stress about me."

His dad looked up from his pasta and managed a weak smile. "It's good to have a friend, son."

31

Chapter 5

Cody was gazing out of the window the next morning when he saw a delivery person struggle up the path towards his front door. He was carrying an enormous basket of fruit. Cody dashed downstairs, before the man had a chance to ring the doorbell.

"Mr Mather's house?" the man asked.

"Yeah," Cody muttered. "Um … I'll take it, thanks."

"Who is it?" Cody's mum called from the kitchen.

"Nothing," Cody called back. "A mistake." Cody grabbed the card sticking out from a pineapple and quickly read it.

*Wishing you
a speedy recovery,
from the Maclean family*

Maclean was his friend Max's family name! Max must have told his parents! Cody stuffed the card in his jeans pocket and hurriedly manoeuvred the fruit basket upstairs and into his room without his mum seeing. It was the biggest fruit basket he'd ever set eyes upon.

He emptied the contents of his rucksack on the floor then stuffed it with apples, oranges, peaches, grapes, nectarines, kiwi fruits, cherries and bananas. The pineapple was too big. He pushed that under his bed. Five minutes later, he was heading out of the house, his rucksack weighing more than it ever did with schoolbooks in it.

Like Cody knew he would be, Alfie was in the park waiting for him. With all the fruit business, Cody had forgotten the football.

"No worries," said Alfie, grinning. "There are plenty of other things we can do, like the climbing wall, skimming stones down at the river, doing target practice. Loads!"

"I brought a picnic," Cody said.

Alfie was practically jumping up and down he was that excited. They headed for the climbing wall and managed to get right to the top. Then they wandered down to the river, which skirted the edge of the park.

"I love the river," Alfie said. "Sometimes me and my dad come here and do some fishing. And he knows the names of all the birds."

"What's that one?" Cody pointed to a large grey bird poised at the edge of the river.

"Heron," said Alfie. "It flies away when I skim stones. My record is 14."

"Impressive," Cody said, setting the heavy rucksack down and starting to gather flat smooth stones.

For the next hour or so, that's what they did. Ducks flew up and flapped away. The boys skimmed stones and watched them bounce over the surface of the water. Cody might be champion footballer, but Alfie was definitely champion skimmer.

"You like fruit, Alfie?" Nodding, Alfie plonked himself down next to Cody, who was unclipping his rucksack. Out tumbled bananas, apples and bright red cherries. "Good," Cody went on, holding up a peach, "because I've got loads!"

They stuffed their faces.

It was when Cody reached in his bag to fish out a hairy kiwi fruit that the card fell from his pocket. Alfie saw the words, scrawled in loopy handwriting.

"You not well?" Alfie asked, ready to bite into a green apple.

Cody felt his cheeks flame. He was sick of lying, sick of pretending. "It's my dad," he muttered. "He's … um – "

A goldeneye duck landed in the river. In the distance, a dog barked. Cody threw his apple core away.

"His business crashed and so we've no money and we're supposed to be in Spain right now, then Aviemore, then Skye, but everything got cancelled, because my dad lost all his money."

"That's a shame," Alfie said.

"Yeah, I don't even have a phone anymore. And I've got nothing to do. I'm like this poor boy."

"But you've got lots of fruit."

"Yeah, well, that's a lie. I told Max my dad wasn't well. Like, it was a big excuse. And suddenly all this fruit arrives."

Alfie giggled. Cody glared at him. "It's not funny."

But Alfie couldn't stop laughing. "I know," he said, cracking up laughing. "I can't … help it."

There's something catching about laughing and soon Cody was joining in. "You'll never guess what else," Cody said, whimpering with laughter, "there's a pineapple under my bed!"

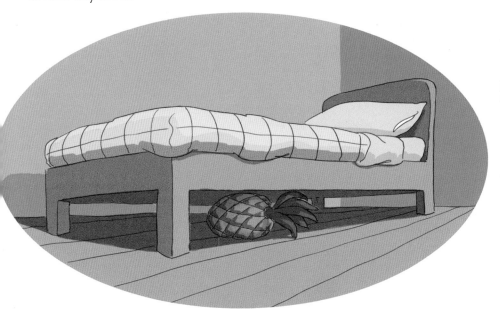

Alfie rolled backwards, hooting with laughter. "A pineapple?" Alfie cried, holding his sides. "Under your bed?" They laughed so much that tears streamed down their faces. Because suddenly a pineapple under a bed seemed like the funniest thing in the world.

"It's not a total lie anyway," Alfie said, lying on his back and still laughing. "I mean, your dad probably *doesn't* feel great." He grinned at Cody. "You could always give him the pineapple!"

Chapter 6

Cody and Alfie fell into a summer routine: meeting
up in the park in the morning, doing the rounds of
the swings, climbing wall and roundabout, then drifting
down to the river to skim stones and, when it was hot,
paddle and splash about. On some days, Cody brought
his football along, and sometimes they made up teams
with other children. Sometimes Angus was there, and
a few others from school that Cody didn't know well.
Not everybody, he realised, was off sunning themselves
in Spain.

But mostly the football stayed at home.

It was after two weeks, on a day when the sun had disappeared behind thick clouds, that they discovered the old fishing hut. They had been wandering further, Alfie pointing out river birds and ducks, like coots, goldeneye and cormorants.

"What's that?" Cody said, pointing, not at a bird this time, but at an old wooden hut behind a clump of birch and rowan trees near the riverbank.

Alfie shrugged. They approached the hut, camouflaged amongst the leafy trees. There was one broken window, and they peered inside.

"It's empty," Cody announced, then squinting his eyes, added, "apart from some old newspapers."

"And a bench," Alfie said, "and a tin cup."

They glanced at each other, then nodded, as if they knew what each other was thinking.

They crept round the side of the hut and came to the rusty old door. Alfie tried turning the doorknob. "It's stuck," he said, but after a nudge with his shoulder, it suddenly swung open, creaking loudly. "We can make it our den," Alfie said, inside now and gazing about.

"Looks like nobody's been here for years."
Cody whistled, picking up a jar of coffee from the ground.
"Best before July 1998," he read. "Wow! This place is
seriously ancient!"

Alfie was examining one of the magazines, yellow
with age. "Fishing in Scotland, November 1986," he read.
"Wow, this place is like a museum." Alfie sat down
on the bench, grinned and looked at Cody. "And we
discovered it! Welcome to 'Home sweet home'."

The next day, the old fishing hut began to resemble home sweet home. Alfie brought a tartan blanket from his bed and draped it over the bench. Cody brought a poster of Esk Valley Rovers football team, and pinned it to the wall. He brought a cushion from his bedroom and propped that against the wall.

"Nice," Alfie said, looking around approvingly. "I could live here. I could get a sleeping bag, and a candle for when it's dark. I could stay here all the time."

"Me too," Cody said.

"And I wouldn't have to move anymore," Alfie went on, reaching into the plastic bag he'd brought with him. He lifted out a wooden box. "You play chess, Cody?"

When Cody didn't immediately answer, Alfie smiled. "No worries, I'll teach you. My dad taught me."

He opened the board of black and white squares, set it carefully on the ground, then started placing the small wooden pieces onto the squares. "That's a pawn. They guard the front line. And this," he said, showing Cody a small carving of a rearing horse, "is my favourite. He's the knight."

While the rain pattered gently on the window, Alfie taught Cody how to play chess. And neither of them was in any hurry to go home.

Chapter 7

The summer that Cody had dreaded,
since the awful news of his dad's
business, was turning into a summer
way better than he'd imagined.
The days seemed to get better and
better: playing high on the swings,
so high they could see right over
the Firth of Forth to Fife, scrambling
on the climbing wall, birling on
the roundabout, skimming stones,
setting up a tin-can target and trying
to hit it with pebbles, spotting birds
and learning their names, playing
chess, playing football, and then just
hanging out in the den, which grew
cosier and cosier. By the end of July,
it was like an art gallery in there.
They did drawings of houses, birds,
trees, footballers, and cartoon portraits
of each other, and pinned them up.
And they made a sculpture of stones,
balanced precariously one on top of
the other.

47

They were sitting on cushions, munching on crisps that Alfie had brought, tired after running around playing football, when Cody suddenly said, "Sorry, by the way."

Alfie frowned. "For what?"

"Barking at you. Like it was such a big deal."

Alfie held a crisp in the air, still looking confused.

"That football game in school, when you ran onto the pitch," Cody said. "I mean, it was only a game, and I was roaring at you for messing it up like it was such a big deal."

Alfie shrugged. "It's OK, I'm used to it."

"Doesn't mean it's right."

Alfie twisted his dark hair round a finger. "When school starts," he began, tentatively, "will you – ?"

"What?"

"You know – " Alfie chewed his lip.

"Ignore you? Pretend I don't know you?"

Thoughts whirled through Cody's mind. How he'd called the new boy a loser. How most people in school ignored him or laughed at him. How he'd tried so hard to fit in but kept getting things wrong. How Cody never picked him for a team. "Course not," he said, but just for a moment he wondered what Max and the others would say.

A low whining noise reached them, coming from the river.

"What's that?" Alfie jumped up and ran to the window.

Chapter 8

Cody scrambled to his feet, following Alfie to the window. He peered out. "I can't see anything," he said. "It sounds like a baby. Or something in distress."

They ran outside and tracked the pitiful whining noise up the river. "It's a dog," Alfie said, pointing out to the flowing water. "And it's stuck!"

For a few moments, Alfie and Cody just stared, helpless, and the dog, noticing them, stared mournfully back. *Help,* it seemed to say with its frantic whining.

"We can save it," Alfie said, immediately pulling his hoodie over his head and dropping it on the grass.

"How?"

"I don't know. Maybe it's just scared. Maybe it ran in after a stick and now can't get out."

They both looked around, as if whoever threw the stick might suddenly appear. But there was nobody.

"Come on!" Alfie yelled, slipping down the bank and into the river. He was soon ankle deep in the water. The dog seemed to be balanced on a rock, the water splashing over its legs. Alfie took a step deeper towards the dog. Cody scrambled in after him. "It's OK, wee dog," Alfie was saying soothingly, as the dog continued to whine. "It's going to be all right."

"What kind of dog is it?" Cody was shouting.

"A mix," Alfie called back. "I've seen it around. I think it belongs to an old man." Then Alfie focused on trying to comfort the stricken dog.

"I'll get you out safe," he was saying. "It's all right, wee dog, don't you worry, it's all right." Alfie reached forward and touched the dog gently on the leg.

"Hey! Something's swirling in the water next to it," Cody cried. "Look!"

They stared down at what looked like a mangled kite, or part of one, snagged on a rock and wrapped around the dog's leg. "It's trapped," Alfie shouted. "Cody, you comfort the dog. I'll get this stuff off."

Cody waded in up to his knees. The poor dog was trembling. Cody took over Alfie's soothing talk. "It's OK, wee dog, we'll get you out." His voice seemed to calm the dog.

Meanwhile, Alfie plunged his arms under the water and tried to work free the tangled tail of the kite. But it was knotted tight, and every time the dog tried to pull its leg free, it trapped itself further.

"I need a sharp stone," Alfie said, rummaging around in the stony riverbed. He pulled one up. With it, he cut away at the plastic wrapped around the dog's leg. And all the time, Cody patted the dog and muttered words of comfort.

"Got it!" Alfie yelled, and fell back against Cody as the plastic tail of the kite suddenly came free. Aware he was no longer trapped, the dog leapt from the stone onto the riverbank. He shook himself, then sat down, waiting for Cody and Alfie. Now soaked, they both quickly fished around for remaining bits of kite. Then, armed with triangles of soggy pink and orange plastic, they waded out of the river towards the waiting dog.

"You're fine now," Alfie said, stroking the damp dog and drying himself with his hoodie.

"You better go home," Cody said to the dog. The dog looked from Cody to Alfie and softly barked.

Alfie bent down and stroked the dog behind its wet, floppy ears. "You can come and live with me and my dad," he said, then glanced up at Cody. "Is that OK with you?"

"What about the old man?"

Alfie shrugged. "We'd be doing him a favour. I don't think he can cope anymore. And my dad loves dogs."

Chapter 9

Approaching home, Alfie could smell pizza. The way the dog wagged its tail, Alfie was sure it could smell pizza too. Alfie and the dog entered the flat just as Alfie's dad was carrying piping hot pizza to the kitchen table. He stared at his son and the wet dog he had with him. "Another new pal?" The dog was pressed up against Alfie's leg.

"It's OK, boy," Alfie said, patting it reassuringly. "That is my dad and he's a good guy."

"Well, thanks for that, son, but – ?" He gave him a quizzical, what's-going-on look. "And why are you soaked?"

"Me and Cody rescued him. He was tangled up with a kite in the river. Can we keep him? Please?"

During this speech, the dog shifted towards the pizza on the table. With one sudden move, he got up with his front paws, snatched a piece of pizza and wolfed it down.

"Hey!" Alfie's dad yelled. "Stop that!"

Too late. The pizza was gone, and the dog was back, cowering behind Alfie's legs.

"He's probably starving," Alfie said. "It's OK, Dad, that can be my piece of pizza. I don't mind." He bent down to pat the dog. "You've still got yours."

"Look, son. It's great you rescued a dog, but we can't keep it. I told you before. Not the way things are. And in rented flats, they're not keen on pets. And Ella isn't keen on dogs." He cut the remaining piece of pizza in two and handed Alfie half. "For you, son, not the dog."

"Please, can I keep the dog? It can sleep in my room, and I'll take it for walks. Please?"

Eyeing the dog, Alfie's dad ate his pizza. "No, and anyway, it probably belongs to someone."

"Yeah, an old man, and he can't even bend to pick up after the dog. I've seen him in the park. We'd be doing him a big favour."

Alfie's dad shook his head. "Sorry, son. Maybe one day, when things are different, we'll get a dog. But not now. I'll check out where the nearest dog rescue centre is, and we'll take him there."

Alfie made a whimpering noise, a bit like the dog. "It's not fair."

"Look, son. Change out of these wet clothes. Then you can play with him in your room for a bit, but we'll have to take him to the cat and dog home. He can't stay here."

Alfie fed the rest of his pizza to the dog, while his dad made himself toast. Later, while Alfie's dad was looking up directions for the animal rescue centre, Alfie found a tie, made it into a lead for the dog, then crept out of the flat, coaxing it gently. "Come on, pal," he murmured, "let's go for a wee walk." Quietly, he shut the front door. Next moment, they were running down the street, heading for the park. He let the dog free and it skipped and circled around him, wagging its tail and barking excitedly. Alfie threw sticks and the dog bounded after them. It was when the dog slowed down, panting like it was exhausted, that Alfie had the idea to go to the den.

"You can stay there for ever," Alfie said, heading now up the river with the dog at his heels. "Come on!"

Inside the hut, it looked cosy. Evening sun slanted
through the window giving everything inside a warm
orange glow. Cushions and blankets were scattered around.
There were still some crisps in a bowl from the afternoon.
Immediately, the dog settled itself on a soft cushion.
Alfie snuggled in next to it.

He reached for a magazine. "I'll tell you a story,"
Alfie said, soothingly, stroking the dog with one hand and
flipping open the magazine with the other. "All about
fishing for salmon in the River Tweed!"

Meanwhile, Cody was slumped on the sofa at home watching TV, his mum on one side of him, his dad on the other. The programme was supposed to be a comedy but nobody was laughing. Cody couldn't stop thinking about Alfie and the dog. Something was up, he felt sure. It was eight o'clock at night, but still light outside. Restless, Cody got to his feet. His parents were glued to the TV and didn't notice. Sure that something was wrong with Alfie, Cody slipped outside.

It felt good to get away from the house. He ran to the park, half expecting to find Alfie on the swings. But the park was empty. Cody ran to the river. Still there was nobody around. Next thing, his feet took him in the direction of the den. It stood, in shadow, hidden by the trees.

Cody approached the den and peered in through the window. There was Alfie and the dog, both of them asleep on the cushions. Cody remembered what Alfie had called it – home sweet home.

Cody carefully opened the door so as not to disturb them, but the dog whimpered, then barked like a guard dog. That woke Alfie. He looked up at Cody and beamed. "Me and the dog have run away," he announced. "This way I don't have to keep changing schools." He yawned. Cody sat down next to them. "And I can be in your team," Alfie went on.

It was getting dark in the hut. "Shame we don't have a candle," Cody said, pulling the blanket over his shoulders.

The two of them sat in silence, watching the night fall. The dog was asleep between them, making contented little snores. It felt cosy and peaceful in there and soon Alfie and Cody were asleep too.

Chapter 10

"So, they have this nightly boarding service. Looks like we have to pay for it. Then they team up with East Lothian council and the police, to try and reunite the lost pet with the owner." Alfie's dad was reading this information off his laptop, calling through from the kitchen. "So they'll sort it. The old man is probably worried sick." He closed his laptop and shook his car keys. "Right son, let's get going."

When there was no response, he went through to Alfie's room and flicked on the bedroom light. There was no sign of Alfie, or the dog. "Alfie?" He pulled back the duvet. Then he peered under the bed. "Alfie, where are you?"

He ran back into the kitchen, then into the living room. He looked in the bathroom, and in the cupboard. He ran into his own bedroom, then bolted over to the window and stared down to the street below. It was starting to get dark.

He grabbed his jacket and dashed outside. "Alfie!" he shouted. Someone opened a door. "My boy," Alfie's dad called over to them. "Did you see a boy, dark hair, skinny, with a dog? Did you see him? He's 12."

"Sorry," the woman called back.

Alfie's dad tore off down the street. His first thought was to make for the park. Alfie was always in the park. He ran faster, hoping against hope he would find him there. "Alfie!" he shouted, approaching the big gates of the park. They were shut. He yanked at the large handle, then saw the sign.

He peered through the railings, then scaled the gates, jumping down and rolling on the grass. Now he ran through the empty park, the moon rising behind the pine trees. He ran to the swings. Alfie loved the swings. But nobody was there. The swings creaked in the breeze. Alfie's dad looked frantically around. He called his son's name, then waited. But all he could hear was the thudding of his heart.

At 17 Esk Avenue, Cody's mum switched off the TV. "Where's Cody?"

"He was right here." Cody's dad looked around the room, scratching his head.

"Cody?" His mum called up to his bedroom, then hurried up there, to find the room empty. "He's gone!" she called out, a panic rising in her voice. "And he doesn't even have a phone. He's probably gone to his friend's house, Alfie. We don't even know where he lives."

"Right," her husband said, "let's go and look for him. We can't just stand here fretting."

"The river," Cody's mum said, as they hurried down the street. "He's always going on about the river. Says how they skim stones, and try and catch fish. He says there's lots of swans and ducks on the river." She kept talking, her voice rising with worry.

"I should have paid him more attention," Cody's dad was saying. "I've been so caught up in my own money worries." They reached the river at the back of the park. "Now what?" He looked up to where the twisting river disappeared into the dark woods.

Cody's mum took a deep breath, then at the top of her voice called out, "CODY!" She squeezed her husband's arm. "Listen," she whispered.

"What?"

"A dog whining. Can you hear? Didn't Cody say something about a dog?"

They stood, straining to listen. Sure enough, through the darkness came the low, mournful sound of an animal whining. "Let's follow it," Cody's mum said.

At the edge of the park, Alfie's dad heard it too.
He wriggled through a thick hedge, then burst out at
the other side and ran along the riverside, following the cry
of the dog.

Which was how all three adults, breathless and sick with
worry, ended up outside the hut. "Alfie's dad?" Mrs Mather
asked, panting hard.

Alfie's dad nodded. "Cody's parents?"

They nodded and then, with trepidation, approached
the door of the hut. Alfie's dad shone the torchlight from his
phone, while Cody's dad turned the handle.

"Oh, thank goodness," Mrs Mather sobbed, as Alfie's
dad shone the torchlight on two boys, sleeping soundly
in the hut, with tartan blankets over them. For a moment,
the three adults stared in, gratitude and relief washing
over them. "Thank goodness," Mrs Mather kept muttering.
"Thank goodness!"

Entering the hut, Alfie's dad cast the light around. They all saw the pictures on the wall. The stones. The bowls, blankets and cushions. The dog stretched and licked Alfie's face. "Come on, son," his dad said, gently lifting him up.

"You too," Cody's dad said, patting his son on the shoulder. "Let's go home."

"What about the dog?" Alfie murmured, sleepily.

"We can take him for now," Cody's dad said. "Come on, lads, it's time to go home."

Chapter 11

Somehow, things changed after that night in the hut. Maybe it was seeing the pictures on the wall, but Alfie's dad decided they would stay put, for a couple of years at least. When Alfie heard that, he couldn't stop smiling. And Mr Mather tracked down the owner of the dog, who said he would be very happy to share the dog. "His name is Charlie," the old man said, "and if you would take him for walks that would be a grand help to me." Mr Mather said it would be a grand help for him too. "Me and Cody will take him for walks," he said, ruffling his son's hair.

"Alfie can come too," Cody added, beaming.

By the middle of August, when it was time to go back to school, Cody remembered the teacher's summer challenge – *Jump into the new.*

He would have plenty of new things to tell them about. Not the kind of things he thought he would be telling them about. Other children in the class could talk about zorbing, land yachting, bungee jumping, kayaking and sailing, and new Spanish words.

Cody had other new words, like goldeneye, coot, heron, mute swan. Charlie. And Alfie.

Sure enough, there was a lot of excitement in
the classroom about Aviemore. Lots of talk about how
fantastic the land yachting had been.

At the end of his action-packed presentation,
Max looked over at Cody. "We were just sorry Captain
Cody wasn't there, telling us all what to do!" Max laughed.
It was supposed to be a joke but didn't sound like one.

Then it was Cody's turn. Chewing his lower lip, Alfie watched him rise to his feet. The others in the class fell silent.

"So," the teacher said, encouragingly, "tell us about your new."

Cody looked around the room. Everyone waited. Cody took a deep breath, then began. "My dad's business crashed and he lost lots of money, so we couldn't go on holiday, and I was really upset about that, and pretty ashamed, and then – " He looked over at Alfie who was staring down at the desk. "Then I made a great friend and I had the best time ever, and I learnt that team games are not everything, and you can have fun just mucking about, and playing down by the river, and having loads of adventures, and you don't need tons of money. And macaroni cheese is the best."

Morven laughed at that. So did Angus.

"That's wonderful," the teacher said.

"Yes, and we rescued a dog from the river. He's called Charlie. And I just want to say Alfie is my friend and … and I want him to know, he made my summer holidays the best ever. And," Cody went on, "this is his seventh school but he can stay here right to the end of the school year. And he can be in the football team. And I'm really happy he's going to stay."

The teacher started clapping, which set off a round of applause from the whole class.

"Me too," Alfie managed to say. "I'm really happy! And my new is – " A huge smile lit up his face. "I'm not going to a new school!"

Jumping into the new

So the teacher says we should write down all our new things, so we don't forget. Well, mine haven't exactly happened yet, but they will. I know Spain is really great and hot, and the sea is this turquoise blue (we've been before so maybe not exactly new) but actually, I'm most excited about Aviemore. They have everything, like dry skiing, and this new thing called land yachting. Imagine, sailing on the sand!!
Can't wait!
10th June. Cody

Things don't always work out
the way you planned – that's
what our teacher said today.
And she's right. Maybe next year,
I'll go land yachting. Maybe Alfie
could come too. He's never done
any of that stuff. But what I learnt
is that it's OK even when things
don't work out the way you hoped.
It really is OK.
20th August. Cody.

Ideas for reading

Written by Gill Matthews
Primary Literacy Consultant

Reading objectives:

- check that the book makes sense to them, discussing their understanding and exploring the meaning of words in context
- draw inferences such as inferring characters' feelings, thoughts and motives from their actions, and justify inferences with evidence
- discuss and evaluate how authors use language, including figurative language, considering the impact on the reader

Spoken language objectives:

- articulate and justify answers, arguments and opinions
- participate in discussions, presentations, performances, role play, improvisations and debates

Curriculum links: Geography – Locational knowledge; Geographical skills and knowledge

Interest words: blurted, muttered, wandered, shrugging, ambled

Resources: IT, atlas

Build a context for reading

- Ask children to look at the front cover of the book and to read the title. Explore what it means to them.
- Read the back-cover blurb. Ask children why they think Cody's plans might have been cancelled. Discuss how someone might have changed things for Cody.
- Draw attention to this being a contemporary story. Discuss other contemporary stories children have read. Ask what features they expect the story to have.

Understand and apply reading strategies

- Read pp2–7 aloud, using appropriate expression. Ask children what impression they have of Cody. Where do they think the new boy might have gone?
- Ask children to read pp8–13. Discuss what has happened and how Cody is feeling. Ask why children think he couldn't face his friends feeling sorry for him.